The Case of the Berry Burglars

For Whittaker—a little detective with a taste
for berries and big mysteries — *Liam*

I dedicate this book to summer and its bounty
of berries. Please come back soon! — *Aurélie*

West Meadows Detectives

The Case of the Berry Burglars

Written by
Liam O'Donnell

Illustrated by
Aurélie Grand

Owlkids Books

Owlkids Books acknowledges the financial support of the Canada Council for the
Arts, the Ontario Arts Council, the Government of Canada through the Canada
Book Fund (CBF) and the Government of Ontario through the Ontario Media
Development Corporation's Book Initiative for our publishing activities.

Published in Canada by
Owlkids Books Inc.
10 Lower Spadina Avenue
Toronto, ON M5V 2Z2

Published in the United States by
Owlkids Books Inc.
1700 Fourth Street
Berkeley, CA 94710

Cataloguing data available from Library and Archives Canada

ISBN 978-1-77147-306-4

Library of Congress Control Number: 2017961186

Edited by: Debbie Rogosin
Designed by: Alisa Baldwin

Manufactured in Altona, MB, Canada, in April 2018, by Friesens Corporation
Job #239810

A   B   C   D   E   F

Publisher of Chirp, chickaDEE and OWL | Owlkids Books is a division of
www.owlkidsbooks.com

Table of Contents

CHAPTER 1

Hajrah was missing.

I scanned the school playground. It was 8:33 on Wednesday morning. The schoolyard at West Meadows Elementary was already crowded with kids. But Hajrah wasn't there.

She's my best friend. We meet at the school doors every day at 8:30 a.m. I checked my watch again: 8:34. She was four minutes late. Hajrah always tells me if she's going to be late. Today she didn't, and that set my brain buzzing.

I took a deep breath. Going to school without my best friend wasn't a big deal. It's just that I don't like surprises. They can ruin my whole day. And Hajrah not coming to school today would be a surprise.

Just then, someone called my name from the other side of the schoolyard.

It was Hajrah. She waved her arms and jumped up and down.

"Myron!" she called. "Come here!"

The buzzing in my brain went quiet. Hajrah was here. The surprise was over, but it was replaced by a new question: Why does she want me to leave the school doors? Hajrah knew I didn't like changes to my routine. Running across the playground a minute before the entry bell rang was a *big* change.

"Myron! Come here!" she called again.

Hajrah isn't just my best friend. She's also my detective partner. We solve mysteries in our neighborhood. She calls us the West Meadows Detectives. One thing I do know about my detective partner: I can trust her.

I put the evidence together. Hajrah knows I don't like leaving the school doors, but she is asking me to do this anyway. And she's not giving up. That can mean only one thing…

I ran across the playground.

"Have you found a new mystery?"

Hajrah's eyes went big. "It's a messy one."

"I don't like messes," I said.

"You'll like this one." She led me to the far side of the yard. We stopped near the big chain-link fence that runs around the school. "I got here about ten minutes ago. I walked by the school garden, and this is what I saw."

The garden was near the fence. It had been planted by the garden club a few weeks ago. Now it was the middle of June, so the tiny seedlings had grown into leafy green vegetable plants and colorful flowers. But something was wrong. At one end of the garden, leaves had been trampled and stems snapped in two. Something or someone had damaged the plants.

Other kids gathered around. One girl was moving around the flattened plants, snapping pictures with the camera on her phone.

"Glitch got here a few minutes ago," Hajrah said.

"Hey, Myron." Glitch looked up from her phone and waved. Her real name is Danielle, but everyone calls her Glitch because she is so good with computers. "I figured you guys would want a closer look at this mess when we get to class."

Hajrah leaned in close and spoke quietly. "I've asked around, but nobody knows what happened, and none of the garden club members are here right now."

"That's odd." I pulled my notebook from my backpack. "You'd think one of them would be here to check on the plants in the morning."

Hajrah shrugged. "It could be important, or it could be nothing."

I made a note in my book anyway. This early in an investigation, it was hard to tell the difference between important and nothing.

The school bell rang.

"What's going on here?" a loud voice boomed.

We spun to face Mrs. Rainer, our school

principal. She was thin and wrinkled, but her voice was big and loud. Her tiny eyes went wide at the sight of the plants.

"What happened to our beautiful garden?" She shook her head. "I told Ms. Hemenway she needed to protect the plants from raccoons."

"I don't think it was raccoons, Mrs. Rainer," I said. "Not this time."

The principal smiled. "I'm sure you're

convinced there's a mystery afoot, Myron."

"It was definitely a foot, or maybe a bunch of feet." Hajrah hopped to the principal's side. "We can't be sure, but look at all the footprints in the dirt."

"That's not what I meant," Principal Rainer said.

"We're gathering evidence," Hajrah continued, "and putting together a list of suspects for our report."

She saluted Mrs. Rainer.

"I would prefer it if you just went to class," the principal said, sighing. "Ms. Hemenway and the garden club can deal with this mess."

"And we don't have to write a report, Hajrah," I said. "We aren't police officers, and this isn't a TV show."

"It's also not a mystery. It's simply the

nighttime handiwork of a hungry raccoon or a curious dog. Nothing more and nothing less."

Mrs. Rainer turned and walked back to the school.

"This has *got* to be a mystery," Hajrah whispered. "My stomach feels like it's tap-dancing. That's my detective's hunch. It's telling me there is more to this than hungry animals."

"I agree." I hurried after the principal. "Mrs. Rainer!" I called. "You don't understand."

She stopped at the school doors.

"*You're* the one who doesn't understand, Myron." She glared at me with her beady eyes. "There is *no* mystery to solve. There is only a garden to clean up and schoolwork to do. Case closed. Get to class."

Mrs. Rainer walked away. The sound of her heavy shoes echoed down the hall.

Hajrah and Glitch joined me at the doors.

Hajrah's eyes narrowed. "Why are you smiling, Myron?"

"Because Mrs. Rainer knows a lot about running a school," I said, "but she doesn't know a lot about solving mysteries."

"So the case is still open?" Glitch asked.

"Wide open."

CHAPTER 2

Mr. Harpel greeted us at the door to room 15.

"There they are!" Our teacher's voice was loud and full of laughter. "I thought you got lost on your way to school today."

"That's impossible," I said. "We come to school every weekday. We wouldn't get lost."

Mr. Harpel's round face split into a wide grin. He scratched his bushy beard and chuckled.

"Oh, I get it." I grinned back at him. "You're joking."

"That I am, Myron. But you are correct: detectives like you never get lost."

"You got it, Mr. H.!" Hajrah ran into the classroom and tossed aside her backpack. She belly flopped onto her big rubber ball, bounced into the air, and landed with her arms spread out like a gymnast. "We don't get lost—we find things!"

Room 15 was not like a regular classroom. There were only four students, and there were no desks in rows. Instead, we had

tables where we could work on our own. At my table, I had a comfortable chair and lots of mystery books. Hajrah had the large rubber ball so she could bounce and do schoolwork at the same time. She says bouncing helps her think. Glitch's table was always covered in bits of computers and gadgets. She likes to tinker with technology, especially when she gets upset and needs to calm herself down. Lots of things can upset Glitch. The fourth student, Jordan, had a table that was crammed with markers and colored pens. He was drawing when we arrived.

"Were you guys at the school garden?" Jordan stayed focused on his coloring. "I heard that some animals ate all the plants."

Mr. Harpel sighed. "Gardeners are always trying to protect their crops from hungry critters."

He waved for us to join him for our morning meeting. I put my backpack on my table and moved to the carpet. It had yellow and red circles. I sat in the yellow circle closest to my table.

"We don't think it was animals," I said.

"We think there's a mystery." Hajrah hopped over, making frog noises. "And we're going to solve it!"

"I have no doubt you will crack this case, detectives," Mr. Harpel said. "But why don't you think it was just a raccoon or skunk digging for food?"

"Because my stomach says so!" Hajrah flopped onto the carpet.

"Hajrah has a hunch," I said. "And I agree."

"Ah, yes. A detective's gut feeling that something isn't right." Mr. Harpel nodded.

"Listening to that inner voice can be a good idea."

Jordan looked up. "I thought you didn't believe in hunches, Myron."

"This time he does," Hajrah said, "because it's *my* hunch."

"That's not why," I said. "It was something in the garden. The damage seemed odd."

"Odd?" Mr. Harpel said. "What was strange about the damage?"

I shrugged. "I'm not sure."

"Maybe this will help." Glitch turned on the projector. The interactive whiteboard lit up with rows of little square photographs. "I took these before Mrs. Rainer showed up."

"Photos of the garden!" Hajrah jumped to her feet. She touched a square on the screen and made it bigger.

The photograph showed the ground around the damaged plants.

"It's just dirt and squashed plants," Jordan said.

"And lots of footprints," Hajrah added. "Leading in different directions."

"They could be from the members of the garden club, made before the damage was done," I said. "It's impossible to tell which ones belong to the culprit."

"Too bad." Hajrah tapped the next photo and made it bigger.

It showed the whole garden. In one row, plants lay flat and broken.

"The trespasser really didn't like the plants in that part of the garden," Hajrah said. "The other vegetables aren't damaged."

"The flowers look okay, too," Jordan said

from his table.

"You're right!" I looked more closely at the screen.

Unlike the trampled vegetables, the flowers were untouched.

Hajrah tapped her chin and paced in front of the screen. "So the culprit was only interested in wrecking the vegetable plants."

"I knew there was something strange about the damage." I opened my notebook and wrote down this new piece of evidence. "If it was an animal, some of the flowers would have been trampled, too."

"I think they did more than just damage the plants." Glitch walked to the screen and pointed to a pile of soil. "What happened here?"

"There are no plants," Hajrah said. "Just a few holes."

I studied the image. "Three holes, to be precise."

The holes weren't deep, but they could be important.

"It looks like something was growing there," Glitch said. "And then it was dug up."

"That's it!" I said. "I knew there was more to this than damaged plants. This isn't just a case of vandalism."

"It isn't?" Hajrah asked.

"Way bigger," I said. "It's a robbery."

CHAPTER 3

Fifty-three minutes later, the recess bell rang.

Outside, kids bounced balls, scrambled over the climbing frame, and played tag. But Hajrah and I didn't have time for games. We had a mystery to solve.

"Mr. Harpel told me the garden club leaders are meeting this recess to clean up the damage," I said.

The garden club leaders were kids in seventh and eighth grade who helped run the garden.

Ms. Hemenway, the fifth grade teacher, had trained them to work with the younger kids in the club.

Hajrah skipped beside me as we made our way toward the garden.

"If we're lucky, all the leaders will be there," she said. "Hopefully, they'll be able to tell us who might want to damage the garden."

We had just passed the basketball nets when I heard my sister's voice.

"Myron! Wait!"

Alicia hurried toward us. She was with a girl who had short brown hair and glasses.

"Hey, little brother," Alicia said when she caught up to us. "I'm glad I found you. I bet you're searching for the person who damaged the school garden, right?"

Hajrah's mouth hung open. "How did

you know?"

"He's my little brother, Hajrah!" Alicia rolled her eyes. "Myron has been sniffing out mysteries since he was in diapers."

"That's impossible," I said. "Mysteries don't smell."

"But she's right," Hajrah said. "We are investigating what happened in the garden."

Alicia looked at the girl beside her. "See? Didn't I tell you my detective brother and his best friend would be on the case?" She turned back to us. "This is Simone. She's in my class, and she's one of the garden club leaders."

"I want you to find my strawberries," Simone said.

"Strawberries?" Hajrah asked.

"They're mine, and someone took them."

"We were right! This *is* a robbery." Hajrah

twirled around. "What do you mean they were *your* strawberries?"

"All the club leaders are in charge of one section of the garden," Simone explained. "I'm responsible for growing the strawberries."

"We saw three holes in the ground," I said. "Is that where the strawberry plants were?"

Simone nodded. "They were there yesterday evening. I live up the street and checked on the garden after dinner. The strawberries and all the other plants were fine."

"That means the strawberry thief struck sometime in the night or early morning," Hajrah said.

I wrote this in my notebook.

"They were growing so well." Simone sighed. "I was going to harvest some berries for this Saturday's Strawberry Festival at the botanical gardens."

"That's only three days away," I said.

Simone nodded. "Every year, gardeners from all over town bring their berries to show off and share. But I won't be able to represent the school if my plants are missing."

"We'll take the case!" Hajrah announced.

"We're already on the case," I reminded her.

"But we didn't have a client," Hajrah said.

"And now it's official! We have a client, and this is just like a real mystery."

I was about to say that this was *always* a real mystery, but I knew my partner was right. All the best detectives have someone they're solving the mystery for.

"See you later, little brother," Alicia said. "Have fun with your new case." She headed back to the basketball nets.

I ran to catch up with Hajrah and Simone. They were speaking with Ms. Hemenway.

"I'm so sorry about your strawberry plants, Simone. I'm shocked they were dug up and taken away. Who would do such a thing?"

"That's what we're going to find out," I said.

"This is Myron and Hajrah," Simone said. "They're going to help find the person who did this."

"Ah, yes! Our school detectives."
Ms. Hemenway clapped her hands. "It's
a pleasure to meet you. The whole school
knows about your sleuthing skills. Good to
have you on the case."

"Thank you!" Hajrah bowed.

I opened my notebook and wrote
Ms. Hemenway's name at the top of a new
page. "What can you tell us about the damage
to the garden?"

"Well, it seems only the strawberry plants
were taken," Ms. Hemenway said. "Some of
the other plants are a bit trampled, but they
should recover with a little care from the
garden club."

"Do you mind if we talk to the club
leaders?" I asked. "They might be able to tell
us something."

"Be my guest," Ms. Hemenway said.

Two boys stood next to the three holes where Simone's strawberries had been. One of them had dark curly hair. The other wore a pair of gardening gloves that were too big.

"This is Umair," Simone said.

The boy with the curly hair waved.

"And I'm Jessie," the boy in the too-big gloves said. "I think you know my little brother."

"Aaron?" Hajrah said. "He's in our afternoon class. You look like him."

Jessie smiled. "People say that all the time."

"Myron and Hajrah are helping find out who took my strawberry plants," Simone explained.

I wrote Umair's and Jessie's names in my notebook, below Ms. Hemenway's.

"Are you both garden club leaders?" I asked. Simone had told us they were, but I wanted to make sure. Good detectives always double-check their facts.

Jessie answered first. "Yes," he confirmed, "along with Simone."

"Don't forget Lauren." Umair looked to the far end of the garden, where a girl with blonde hair was moving slowly through the flowers.

"Who could ever forget Lauren?" Jessie rolled his eyes. "She's a club leader, but she's really only interested in growing flowers. She doesn't like to look after our vegetable plants or help the younger kids."

"Club leaders help the kids dig in the garden and make sure they don't trample the vegetables," Simone added.

"This whole thing is very weird," Umair said. "Why would someone steal strawberry plants?"

"That's what we're trying to find out," I said.

"I hope you find out soon, before the thief comes back and digs up my tomato plants." Umair inspected the tall plants growing nearby. Several green tomatoes hung from their branches.

"They're looking really good," Simone said.

"It's all thanks to you." Umair smiled. "I trimmed back the lower branches like you suggested. Now more tomatoes appear each day."

Jessie kicked at the holes. "I bet it was just an animal that did this," he said.

Umair shook his head. "No way. An animal wouldn't dig up the entire plant, roots and all, and take it away."

"That's what we were thinking!" Hajrah said. "It must have been a person."

"In that case, my first guess would be Lauren." Jessie looked her way with his eyes narrowed. "Remember how angry she got when Ms. Hemenway wouldn't let her plant her flowers over here?"

"That's right." Umair snapped his fingers as if he had just solved a math problem. "She said this spot got the best sun, so it would be the best place for the flowers."

"Would she really still be mad about that?" I asked.

Jessie nodded. "Lauren really knows how to hold a grudge."

"She can be mean," said Simone.

"Especially if she doesn't get her way," Umair added.

Hajrah checked her watch. "Recess will be over soon. We should talk to her."

"You two go ahead," Simone said. "I'm going to check on the other plants."

As we walked away, Aaron Sanders ran up.

"Hey, Jessie," he called. "Don't forget that Dad is picking us up after lunch so we can visit Mom."

I turned in time to see Jessie scowl at his younger brother.

"I haven't forgotten," he said. "And I told

you to stay away from here. Get lost."

Aaron's smile vanished. He walked away without saying another word.

Hajrah tugged on her braid. "Why are big kids so mean sometimes?" she whispered. "That's one mystery I *really* want to solve."

We hurried over to where Lauren was working in her flower garden.

"Look at this!" She held up a baseball covered in dirt. "I find these in my flowers all the time." She pointed to the baseball diamond in the corner of the schoolyard. "It's those kids and their batting practice. They hit the balls in here and damage my poor delicate flowers."

We asked her if she knew who would want to steal the strawberry plants. Lauren just laughed.

"The baseball team definitely wants to

damage the plants." She tossed the ball out of the garden. "But I don't know who would want to steal them. Those plants are just a bunch of ugly green leaves. I'm surprised the thief didn't take my beautiful flowers."

Hajrah cleared her throat. "We were told you wanted to put your flowers where the strawberries were planted. Is that true?"

Lauren thought for a second, then laughed.

"Oh, that! I remember now. Ms. Hemenway insisted that I plant my flowers over here. I told her the trees in Warbler Woods block the sun in this part of the garden in the afternoon." She pointed to the forest that ran along the edge of the school grounds. "My flowers would be even more beautiful if they were near the tomatoes and getting sun all day."

"We heard you were quite upset about not getting your way," Hajrah said.

Lauren frowned. "Who told you that? Was it Jessie? You can't trust him. Last year, he stole erasers from me all year. He denied it, but on the last day of school, the missing erasers were found hidden in the back of his desk. And even then he claimed someone else had put them there. Never believe anything he says."

I was about to ask another question, but the recess bell rang.

"I guess we're out of time," Lauren said. "It was fun talking to you guys. Little kids are so cute." She started back toward the school. "See you later, mini detectives!"

"We're not *mini* detectives," I shouted. "We're *real* detectives."

But Lauren was too far away to hear. Hajrah stood beside me as I looked at the garden one last time. The plants seemed so peaceful in the morning sun. But next to the tall tomatoes and leafy lettuce lay the trampled plants. Their leaves were broken and squashed into the soil. Definitely not peaceful. The club leaders didn't seem peaceful, either. Last year, Jessie and Lauren had clashed over stolen erasers. This year, could their fight be about plants?

Hajrah turned to me. "What are you thinking, Mr. Real Detective?"

"I'm thinking that someone in the gardening club knows more than they're telling us." We walked toward the school. "And we're going to keep digging until we uncover the truth."

CHAPTER 4

My afternoon classroom was buzzing. It was
supposed to be quiet, but it wasn't.

We had just come in from lunch recess. Now
we were doing silent reading. Everyone had a
book. Some were reading. Others were not.

This was my "regular" classroom with my
"regular" teacher and the "regular" third-
grade kids. "Regular" meant the other kids
were not autistic like me. Hajrah and I came
to this classroom every afternoon. She sat

beside me on a hard plastic chair. She missed her bouncy ball from room 15. The teacher, Ms. Chu, was nice, but some days she was bossy. Today, she was bossy.

She had already snapped at Aaron Sanders because he was taking things out of his desk and stacking them on his chair in a crooked tower.

"Aaron, I told you to put your things away," Ms. Chu said. "You're supposed to be meeting your father in front of the school. He's picking you up every day this week, remember?"

"I know, but I'm looking for something." As Aaron reached into his desk again, he bumped his chair. The tower toppled to the floor.

Ms. Chu hurried over.

"Things will be better when your mom comes home on Friday." She didn't sound angry anymore. "Go meet your father. He'll be waiting."

Aaron pulled something green out of his desk and crumpled it in his hands. He wiped his eyes as he left the classroom.

"Keep reading, everyone," Ms. Chu called as she put the things back in Aaron's desk.

All the kids went back to reading, but the noises didn't stop. Next desk over, Adeela Rashid jammed a pencil into the desktop again and again. It was like a jackhammer in the back of my head. But the noise that bothered me the most was the hum from the PA speaker. No one else could hear it, but I could. Even when Principal Rainer wasn't making announcements, the speaker hummed. The noise made the words on the page of my mystery blur. I cannot read blurred words. I closed my book.

Ms. Chu looked up from her own book. She sighed when she saw that I wasn't reading.

"Myron, ignore the noise from the speaker."

There was no use arguing with her. She couldn't hear it. No one could, except me. Everyone in the class said I was overreacting. Mr. V., the caretaker, had come to fix the speaker, but he found nothing wrong with it. He said the buzzing was so quiet that I should just pretend it wasn't there. But it wasn't quiet to me, and I couldn't ignore it.

"Do you want me to get the quiet earphones?" Hajrah whispered.

"No, thanks," I said. "I'll get them."

I walked to the back of the classroom and took a pair of noise-reduction earphones from a rack by the window. The earphones were big and red and helped to block the buzzing noise. I was about to put them on, but I stopped. Back in this part of the class, there was a noise I *did* want to hear: Cameron and Carter chatting. The two friends were hiding behind two large hardcover books. From her desk, Ms. Chu couldn't hear them. But I could.

"I heard it was someone on the baseball team who trashed the garden," Carter whispered.

"That's what you get when you plant flowers in the middle of the outfield," Cameron snickered.

"My older brother is friends with Paulo, the team captain," Carter said. "He said the

46

players complained to Mrs. Rainer about the garden being in their outfield."

"What did she say?"

Carter shrugged. "She said the garden was just as important as the baseball team, and they all had to share the field."

"I guess Paulo doesn't like sharing." Cameron started to laugh again, but he stopped when he saw his friend's face.

Carter was scowling. And he was looking at me.

"I don't like snoops," he growled. "Are you spying on us, detective?"

I shook my head and held up the earphones. "I was getting these."

"Well, now that you have them, you can get lost!" Cameron hissed.

I hurried back to my seat.

"What's up?" Hajrah whispered. "Why are you smiling?"

"Because we have some new suspects."

"Really?" she gasped. "How many?"

"Enough to make a whole baseball team."

When afternoon recess came, we raced out to look for Paulo. I filled Hajrah in on what I had heard.

"You think Paulo damaged the garden because Cameron and Carter said so?" she asked. "I don't trust those two. They could be lying. They've never been nice to you or me."

"That's true," I said. "But they didn't know I was listening, so I think they were telling the truth. And Lauren said the baseball players keep hitting balls into the garden. She thinks they're doing it on purpose. If Paulo and the other kids on the team don't like having the garden in their outfield, then they have a reason to commit the crime."

"Really?" Hajrah said. "How does stealing strawberry plants solve their problem with the garden?"

"I don't know," I said. "Maybe someone on the team can tell us."

We found Paulo at the baseball diamond. He was hitting balls with some other kids from the team.

"Ask your questions, but I'm not stopping batting practice," he said after we introduced ourselves. "We have a big game this Saturday, and I have to be in top form."

We stood out of the way and watched a short

kid with glasses pitch a ball. Paulo swung and hit it. The ball sailed over the outfield, the school garden, and the fence, before landing in Warbler Woods.

"Home run!" Paulo cheered. He pointed the bat at the pitcher. "You know the deal, Lewis."

"You hit it, I get it," he sighed. "I'll be right back."

Lewis Devi was in my sister's class. She said he was the smallest kid in seventh grade, but also one of the fastest. He ran to the chain-link fence, lifted up a section, crawled under it, and hurried into the woods.

I pulled my notebook from my pocket and opened it to a blank page.

Hajrah turned to Paulo. "We're investigating some vandalism in the school garden. Do you know anything about it?"

"Nope." Paulo shrugged. "But if it means they'll move the garden, then I'm happy it happened."

"Why don't you like having the garden there?" I asked.

"Because this is a baseball field, not a gardening center," Paulo said. "We can't be the best team in the city if we have to share the outfield with a bunch of carrots and flowers."

"Interesting," Hajrah said.

Paulo's eyes narrowed. "You think I trashed the garden, don't you? Well, you're wrong. I didn't touch it."

"We're just eliminating all the possibilities," Hajrah said.

Lewis emerged from the trees with the ball. "Got it!" he shouted.

He crawled back under the fence and

hurried to the pitcher's mound. Paulo swung his bat, ready to hit another home run.

"I think we're done here, kiddies," Paulo said. "I need to practice." He turned his back to us and got ready for Lewis's pitch.

"What do you think?" Hajrah asked as we walked away.

"I think Paulo is wrong," I said.

The crack of his bat behind us announced another home run.

"We're not done. We're just beginning."

CHAPTER 5

Encyclopedia Brown was blue.

He was not supposed to be blue. He was
a character from my new favorite detective
series. He knew so many facts that everybody
called him Encyclopedia. His real name was
Leroy, but only his parents and teachers
called him that. An encyclopedia is a book
filled with facts. I was drawing his picture
for my *Mystery-o-pedia*, which is a book filled
with facts about detectives. But I picked

the wrong colored pencil to draw with, so
Encyclopedia Brown was blue. Whatever color
he was, Encyclopedia Brown was still a great
detective. I wish I could say the same about me.

The mystery of the missing strawberry
plants had me confused. I had been thinking
about it all through dinner, and I still had
questions I couldn't answer. Why would
someone steal strawberries when you can buy
them at the store? Was there something special
about Simone's plants? Would the thief stop at
strawberries? Were Umair's tomato plants next?

I had many questions but only two suspects
so far. The first was Lauren. She was upset that
the strawberries got the best growing spot. She
could have dug up the plants in hopes of being
allowed to move her flowers to their place.
Paulo was the second suspect. The captain of

the school baseball team didn't like having the garden in his team's outfield. It was in the way when they were playing.

Both suspects could have taken the plants, but that wouldn't have solved their problems. Ms. Hemenway wasn't going to let Lauren plant flowers where Simone's strawberries were. That wouldn't be fair to Simone, and Ms. Hemenway seemed like a fair teacher. Also, digging up the strawberries wouldn't get the garden moved like Paulo wanted. Their motives didn't fit the crime. And that was the biggest mystery of this mystery: Why would someone steal strawberry plants—and only strawberry plants—from a garden?

I wished I were more like Encyclopedia Brown. He always knew an important fact that solved the mystery. I needed to know some facts, too. I went into the living room to ask my mom if I could use the computer. I had research to do.

The next morning, Alicia had band practice, so we arrived at school early. She went to the music room. I walked to the garden to have another look at the crime scene.

In the corner of the schoolyard, the baseball team was having a practice. Paulo hit a ball along the ground. The player at second base scooped up the ball. I recognized Umair right away. He was a gardener *and* a baseball player. Maybe he wanted the garden moved, too. I pulled out my notebook and added this new information to my Suspects page.

I found Simone in the garden. She was digging around the holes where her strawberry plants had been. She waved and held up a handful of dark earth.

"Smell this!" she said.

I stepped back. "I don't want to smell dirt."

"It's not dirt, Myron." She laughed. "This is soil. It's fresh from the ground. Dirt is lifeless. It's just ground-up rocks and minerals."

"Soil contains decaying plant matter, bacteria, fungi, and other forms of life," I said.

"That's right." Simone let the soil fall between her fingers. "How did you know that? I thought you were a detective, not a gardener."

"I am a detective," I replied. "I read about gardens last night. The bacteria and fungi in the soil help plants grow."

My research last night had filled my brain with a lot of facts about gardens.

Simone dug up another handful of soil. "Ever wonder what it smells like?"

"No," I said. "I haven't wondered about soil before."

Simone brought her hands close to her face and sniffed. "I smell strawberries."

"Strawberries?"

She nodded. "Some berries must have been mushed into the soil. I love the smell of strawberries. I can smell them from far away. We can learn a lot if we use all our senses, not just our eyes and ears."

"My senses feel like they're on overload all the time." I thought about the noise from the PA system in my afternoon class.

"I know what you mean." Simone dug her hands into the soil again.

"I'm not sure you do," I said.

"Trust me, Myron. I know exactly what you mean." Her hands stayed buried in the soil. "I'm autistic, just like you. Your sister told me. I hope that's okay."

"It's fine," I said. "I've just never met an autistic girl before."

Simone shrugged. "We're here." She slowly pulled her hands out of the soil and watched the clumps fall to the ground. A second later, she pushed her hands back into the soil again. "This feels nice."

I sat down beside her and stuck my hands into the soil, too. Suddenly, they were wrapped in a heavy cool. It reminded me of crawling under a heavy blanket. It did feel nice.

"When the weather is warm, I come here every morning and dig in the dirt." Simone's voice grew soft. "It helps me get ready."

"Ready for what?"

She nodded toward the school. "To go in there. Some days it's just so loud, it feels like my head will burst."

I thought about the PA again. "And the noise doesn't bother anyone else, right?"

"You got it," Simone said. "No one else thinks the sounds are loud, so they tell you to ignore them. But that's like asking someone to ignore the heat when they're standing in the middle of a volcano."

"So what do you do?"

"This." She pushed her hands deeper into the soil.

I dug deeper, too. The weight of the earth pushed down on my hands. We sat and said nothing for a long time.

The sound of footsteps pulled me away from my thoughts.

"Hi, guys!" Hajrah sat on the ground beside me. Her eyes darted to the edge of the garden. "I don't want to upset you, and this looks like fun, but some kids are staring at you and laughing."

I looked around. Everyone had arrived for school while Simone and I had our arms deep in the soil. Now several older kids were pointing at us and giggling. Hajrah was right; they were laughing at us. In the group, I spotted Lauren. She was laughing, too. She turned away quickly when she saw me looking at her.

My face burned. I wanted to pull my arms out of the soil, run away, and never return to the garden again. But I didn't. Instead, I looked at Simone. She hadn't pulled her arms out. She didn't even look around. She just closed her eyes and dug her arms in deeper.

"People will always stare, Myron," she said. "And they will always laugh. Even when you try to be what they want you to be, they find a reason to laugh at you. Some people are missing out on so much, and they don't even know it."

Hajrah stared at the older kids. Then she turned to Simone and smiled.

"I like you, Simone." My detective partner rolled up her sleeves and dug her arms deep into the soil. "Oh, that feels nice."

We sat in silence with our arms in the soil until the bell rang. When we got up to go inside, I had never felt more relaxed and ready for school.

CHAPTER 6

By the time we got inside, the hallways were empty, except for a few stragglers like us. Principal Rainer was in front of the office. She was talking to a small man wearing an old blue raincoat and green rubber boots. Hajrah rushed past the office, but I stopped. Dark-colored dirt covered the man's boots.

"Something must be done!" he said in a raspy voice.

Principal Rainer smiled at him. "Tell me

what happened, Mr. Bohdan."

Mr. Bohdan cleared his throat. "Last night, some kids from this school snuck into my backyard. I saw them from my kitchen window. By the time I got outside, they were already gone—and so were some of my plants. Roots and all!"

A shock ran through me.

"Were they strawberry plants?"

Principal Rainer and Mr. Bohdan looked at me.

"Yes, they were," Mr. Bohdan said. "How on earth did you know that? Are you the plant thief?"

"No," I said. "I'm a detective."

Principal Rainer chuckled. "This is Myron. He's one of our students—and an accomplished mystery solver."

Footsteps sounded down the hall behind me.

"And I'm Hajrah!" my detective partner called. She ran up beside me and waved to Mr. Bohdan. "I'm accomplished, too."

"Well, if you can both get my strawberry plants back, I would be very grateful."

"It seems you were right, detectives. We *do* have a mystery on our hands. Mr. Bohdan lives next door to the school." Principal Rainer turned to him. "How do you know the children you saw were from West Meadows?"

"Simple." Mr. Bohdan pulled something from his pocket. He handed it to Principal Rainer. "One of the thieves dropped this."

It was a green baseball cap. On the front, stitched in gold letters, was the name of our school.

"Another clue!" Hajrah stopped mid-bounce. "Wait a minute. Did you say *one* of the thieves?"

Mr. Bohdan nodded. "I saw two sneaking around my garden last night."

Hajrah spun to face me. "That means we're looking for more than one culprit. If we find the owner of the hat, we find the berry burglars!"

"That might be difficult," Principal Rainer said. "Every student in the school received one of those hats at the start of the year."

"Oh, yeah." Hajrah's shoulders slumped. "We got them on Spirit Day."

"I didn't get a hat," I said.

"Yes, you did," Hajrah said. "You said it made your head itch, so you didn't even take it home."

"I remember now. It was itchy. And I don't like the color. That green makes my stomach churn."

"Okay," Hajrah said. "But the hat proves that at least one of the burglars is a student at our school."

Principal Rainer turned the hat over. "There's no name written inside it, so your search will have to continue."

Questions ran through my mind. Did the hat belong to Paulo or someone else from the baseball team? Or maybe Lauren from the garden club? Even if it did belong to one of them, the motives still didn't make sense.

Why steal strawberry plants from an old man's garden? Taking Mr. Bohdan's plants wouldn't get the school garden moved, like Paulo wanted. And it wouldn't help Lauren get her flowers into the sunniest spot. The two thefts had to be connected, but how? We were missing something. I needed to know more.

"Will you be home this morning?" I asked Mr. Bohdan.

"I suppose. Nothing else planned for the day."

"Please don't move anything in your garden," I said. "We'll be in touch very soon."

I walked quickly down the hall toward room 15. Hajrah fell into step beside me.

"What have you got planned, Mr. Detective?" she asked.

"If Mr. Harpel says it's okay, I'm hoping we can investigate our new crime scene."

Mr. Harpel thought it was a great idea. Thirty-seven minutes later, we were all standing with Mr. Bohdan in his garden.

"Don't worry, Mr. Bohdan," Hajrah said when we arrived. "We are here as detectives, not just a bunch of kids."

"We're still kids, Hajrah," I said.

"True." She nodded. "So we're here as detectives *and* kids. But we won't goof around. Promise."

"Thank you for letting us visit your garden on such short notice, Mr. Bohdan," said Mr. Harpel. "When Myron and Hajrah arrived at class so excited, I couldn't say no to their suggestion of a field trip."

"A field trip to the house next door to the

school?" Mr. Bohdan scratched his head. "Not much of a trip, if you ask me. But if it gets my plants back, I'll be happy."

Mr. Bohdan's backyard was a rectangle with a tall wooden fence running along the two longest sides. Our school was on the other side of one of the fences. At the back of the yard, there was a low chain-link fence. On the other side was Warbler Woods. An iron gate hung open in the middle of the fence. Beyond it, a path led into the woods. Hajrah stood near the gate, sniffing some purple flowers.

Vegetable plants of all sizes grew in straight rows all the way to the back fence.

"The strawberry plants are this way." Mr. Bohdan walked between the rows. "I should say they *were* this way. They were growing beautifully. This is prime strawberry season, so they were red, ripe, and ready to eat."

"Maybe the thieves took them because they were so ripe," Glitch suggested.

"Why couldn't they grow their own berries?" Mr. Bohdan said. "I was going to bring some to the Strawberry Festival this weekend."

He stopped beside three holes close together in the soil. A small strawberry plant grew next to the holes.

"These holes are about the same size as the ones in the school garden," I said. "And you still have one strawberry plant left."

"It's the smallest plant with the fewest berries!" Mr. Bohdan snorted. "The thieves took my three best plants, roots and all. Those scoundrels better replant them quickly so

they survive."

Glitch walked slowly around the holes and took photos. Jordan drew a map of Mr. Bohdan's garden in his sketchbook. I opened my notebook to a blank page and got my pencil ready.

"Tell us about what you saw, Mr. Bohdan."

"It was around ten o'clock. I was just heading to bed when I saw them from my kitchen window. There were two of them moving through my plants. I rushed out to see what they were up to. But I don't move so fast these days. By the time I got here, they had the plants dug up and had carried them through the back gate into the woods."

"Could you describe them?" I asked.

"It was dark, so all I could see were shapes moving in the garden." Mr. Bohdan paused.

"There's one red-haired girl who likes causing trouble in those woods. She usually shows up with two boys about your age, Myron. The girl has a dog, too. Little spotted thing. They all throw sticks into my garden and then send the mutt in to fetch them. That dog tramples my vegetables and barks as if its tail is on fire. They think it's funny. And they just laugh when I tell them to scram."

My throat went dry. There was only one girl at our school who fit that description: Smasher McGintley. And the two boys sounded like Cameron and Carter. They were always tagging along with Smasher and doing her dirty work. If those bullies were wrapped up in this mystery, I wouldn't be surprised. I would be scared.

Mr. Bohdan walked to the gate.

"I found the hat right here," he said.

The ground around the gate was muddy and churned up with footprints.

"Did you follow them into the woods?" I asked.

"No. I was in my slippers and it can get quite muddy in there." The old man winked. "Besides, once I saw the hat, I knew where to find them."

A flash on the ground caught my eye. I bent down and pulled a small piece of metal from the mud. I wiped it clean and held it out for the others to see. It was the size of a button and had a sharp piece sticking out the back.

"Looks like a pin," Jordan said as he joined us at the gate. "The kind you put on a backpack or a jacket."

"Or a hat," I said.

Mr. Bohdan leaned in to get a closer look. "It doesn't belong to me. I've never seen it before."

The front of the pin had a picture of a tree with the letters "J.G.C." printed underneath.

Jordan studied the pin. "'J.G.C.'? What does that stand for?"

"Maybe it's the thief's initials!" Glitch said.

"Could be," I agreed. "What do you think, Hajrah?"

My detective partner didn't answer. She wasn't in the yard.

"Um, where's Hajrah?"

"A very good question," Mr. Harpel said.

He called her name. A second later, we heard her voice from somewhere in the woods.

"I'm in here! You guys have to see this!"

I stepped through the gate into the dark forest. The others followed.

The path wound its way through the trees. A few steps into the forest, it was blocked by a piece of wide yellow tape. The word "Beware!" and pictures of scary-looking bats were printed on it in a repeating pattern. Hajrah stood next to a tree, tying the tape off with a knot.

"Be careful where you step," she called. "You won't believe what I found!"

"Is that the tape from our Halloween party?" Mr. Harpel asked.

"We had some left over," Hajrah said, "so I thought I'd bring it. And I'm glad I did. Look at that!"

Mr. Bohdan was right—it did get muddy in these woods. Beyond the gate, a narrow rut cut a straight line into the wet ground and joined another path farther into the woods.

Glitch moved in and took photos of the rut. "It looks like the track made by the wheel of a bike."

"That's what I was thinking!" Hajrah said. "And check out what's next to the track mark."

On either side of the rut were several shoe-shaped depressions.

"Footprints!" Jordan bent down and studied them.

"I bet they belong to the burglars," Hajrah said.

Jordan looked up and smiled. "I think I can make a cast of these footprints with the art supplies in the classroom."

"I was hoping you'd say that!" Hajrah clapped her hands as if she'd just won a prize. "Detectives always do stuff like that."

Hajrah was right. We were being detectives and not just kids. If we could match the footprints with a garden club member or baseball player, we would have one of the thieves. With each clue we found, we were getting closer to catching the berry burglars.

CHAPTER 7

It was almost time for recess when we got back to the school.

Jordan and Glitch ran ahead with Mr. Harpel to prepare the plaster of paris to make the cast of the footprints. Hajrah and I trailed behind. We were reviewing our notes from the investigation.

We got to the school just as a red car pulled up. A man climbed out from the driver's side. Jessie and Aaron Sanders climbed out from the back. They both looked as if they had just got out of bed.

"Hurry up, you two," the man grumbled. "You're already late for school, and I'm going to be late for work."

"Relax, Dad." Aaron yawned as he pulled his backpack from the car.

"We're coming," Jessie added, but only after he let out a big yawn, too.

Mr. Sanders glared at his sons.

"Don't you tell me to relax! I'm not the one who couldn't wake up for school this morning. You're both tired because you stayed up late playing video games while I was at the hospital with your mom. I trusted you both to go to bed on time."

The two boys mumbled an apology as they walked past us and followed him into the school.

"Now we know why Aaron keeps falling asleep in class," Hajrah said.

I had heard Aaron snore through a few math lessons recently. Ms. Chu had let him sleep because she thought he was tired from visiting his mother in the hospital. If she knew he was up late playing video games, I don't think she'd be so understanding.

Hajrah opened the school door. "We'd better hurry, too. Mr. Harpel will think we got lost."

"That's unlikely," I said. "We only went next door."

Hajrah twirled in the wide hallway with her arms stretched out. "We could have been waylaid by pirates in the parking lot!"

"That's impossible."

"I know!" Hajrah laughed and raced down

the hall. "That's what makes it funny!"

She ran around the corner. I smiled. Hajrah was right—pirates in the parking lot *was* funny.

Simone turned the little pin over in her hand.

"Junior Growers' Club."

"That's what 'J.G.C.' stands for?" I asked.

Simone nodded. "The Junior Growers' Club is an after-school gardening club for younger kids."

As soon as the recess bell rang, Hajrah and I had searched for Simone. We found her alone in the garden.

Around us, the chaos of recess was in full swing. Kids ran around the schoolyard, chasing each other and shouting. But one step into the garden and I understood why Simone went there every chance she could. Just being near the growing plants calmed my brain. I remembered the cool weight of the soil on my arms. I breathed deeply and listened as Hajrah told Simone about Mr. Bohdan, his missing plants, and what we'd found. When

we showed her the pin, she recognized it immediately.

"I used to be in the Junior Growers' Club," she said. "It meets once a week at the West Meadows

Botanical Gardens."

"The gardens in the middle of Gander Park? With all the rare flowers?" Hajrah asked. "My mom takes me there sometimes on the weekend."

"Do you know what day the club meets?" I asked.

Simone thought for a moment. "I think it's every Thursday after school."

"That's today!" Hajrah spun to face me. "We should totally go, Myron. If we see someone from school, we'll know they're one of the berry burglars!"

"You mean, we'll know they *might* be one of the berry burglars," I said. "Whoever dropped the pin might not be a member of the club anymore."

"That's true," Simone said. "I have a bunch

of those pins. I got one each year I belonged to the club."

"We need to check it out." Hajrah twisted her braid around her fingers.

"How?" I said. "We'd need someone to drive us there."

"My mom!" Hajrah's eyes went wide. "She was just saying that we haven't been to the gardens in a while. She'll be happy to take us!"

Hajrah was right. Her mom was thrilled that we wanted to visit the botanical gardens.

"What a lovely place to go after school," Mrs. Badour said when we arrived at Gander Park. She was a small lady with large glasses that made her eyes look twice as big as they really were.

Hajrah and I had phoned our parents at lunch to arrange the trip. Mrs. Badour agreed to take us right away. My mom said she was happy I was taking an interest in something other than mysteries. I explained that this trip was because of a mystery, but she said that she was still happy and that I should just make sure to be home in time for dinner.

The botanical gardens stood in the middle of Gander Park under two tall glass domes. They were giant greenhouses. In front of the greenhouses was the visitor center. It was a regular building with walls, windows, and a flat roof. Colorful flowers grew along the path leading to the visitor center.

The closer we got to the gardens, the faster

Simone walked.

"It's Thursday, so Eric should be working. He's nice." Simone opened the door to the visitor center, and we stepped inside.

It was busy. People of all ages moved around, chatting and laughing. Their voices carried through the space and bounced off the walls. A café sold snacks and drinks. The coffee machine roared like a monster. Metal spoons banged against cups. Chairs screeched against the tiled floor. Each noise felt like it was happening inside my brain. I wanted to run back outside, but my legs wouldn't move.

I took a deep breath. I had a mystery to solve. Questions needed to be answered. Was one of the burglars a member of the Junior Growers' Club? Was the thief here at the gardens right now? The unanswered questions

drummed more loudly in my mind than the
noises from the café. I forced my legs to move.
I hurried past the noisy coffee shop and the
chatting people and joined Simone near the
reception desk. She looked around the room
and frowned.

"I don't like this area, either, Myron," she
said. "Too many people. Too much noise."

"Let's find the Junior Growers' Club so we
can leave," I said.

Hajrah and her mom were reading a
chalkboard with the day's activities written
in large letters.

"The club is meeting in the vegetable
garden," Hajrah announced.

"Good," Simone said. "It's much quieter
there."

The vegetable garden was behind the

greenhouses. Rows of lettuce and tomatoes
grew in the dark soil. Children about my
age worked in the garden. They all wore the
same green T-shirts with the words "Junior
Growers' Club" written on the back.

"This is it!" Hajrah whispered. "If any of the
kids here go to our school, then we have found
the berry burglars!"

"We *might* have found the burglars," I
corrected. "Just because they're here doesn't

mean they dropped that pin in Mr. Bohdan's garden last night."

"You're right, but it would be quite a coincidence." Hajrah studied the gardeners closely, then shook her head. "None of these kids go to our school."

"I don't recognize anyone, either," Simone said.

"Maybe coming here wasn't such a good idea," Hajrah grumbled.

She was right. It seemed the pin we found in Mr. Bohdan's garden was a dead end.

A teenager in a green T-shirt saw us watching. He had a badge pinned to his shirt that read, "Eric, J.G.C. Leader." He smiled when he saw Simone.

"Hey, Simone! Good to see you."

"Hi, Eric." She waved. "We're looking for someone."

"A friend?" Eric asked.

"A thief!" Hajrah said. "We're detectives. We're looking for some strawberry burglars."

"Isn't everyone?" Eric laughed. "That's all they're talking about inside at the seed swap meeting. A bunch of folks had their strawberry plants dug up in the middle of the night."

Hajrah's eyes locked on to mine. "I knew coming here was a good idea!"

"You just said it was a bad idea," I reminded her.

Hajrah rolled her eyes. "Never mind what I said. We need to get to that seed swap!"

We raced back inside to the meeting room, where gardeners from all over town had gathered. Tables were covered with little boxes filled with tiny seeds. Near each table, gardeners stood chatting, laughing, and trading seeds.

"I haven't been to a seed swap in ages," Mrs. Badour said. "They're a great way to meet other gardeners and get new seeds for your garden."

"It looks like fun," Hajrah said.

I stopped at the door to the meeting room. "It looks loud."

"Very loud." Simone stepped away from the doors.

Hajrah took her mom's hand.

"Stay here, guys. Let us deal with this one."

I handed her my notebook. "Make sure you get the names and addresses of everyone who has had their strawberries stolen."

"Yes, sir!" Hajrah saluted and skipped into the room with her mom.

I watched my detective partner bounce
from one group of gardeners to the next.
Mrs. Badour tried to keep up, but eventually
she stopped and chatted with a young couple
in checkered shirts.

Beside me, Simone spun around suddenly and
sniffed the air.

"Strawberries!" she announced, and she
hurried away.

I followed her but didn't say anything. She
was too focused. With every step, she sniffed
the air. Soon we were both running through
the visitor center. We stopped in front of a long
plastic table set with small bowls, spoons, and
a large container of red fruit.

"I knew I smelled strawberries," Simone said.

"There's fresh cream, too." A lady with curly
gray hair walked over to the table. She carried

a large metal bowl filled with whipped cream. "Only one dollar a bowl."

A younger lady in glasses carried over another bowl of cut strawberries. "We're raising money for our dear friend Angie. She's quite ill."

"She's a keen gardener and loves strawberries," the lady with curly hair added. "This time every year, her backyard is usually bursting with bright red berries. She grows the juiciest ones in town."

"It's sad to think of what her garden must look like this year." The lady in glasses sighed. "Poor Angie has been in the hospital such a long time."

"She comes home this Friday, and we wanted to present her with a gift," the curly-haired lady said. "So we've brought berries

from our gardens to help raise money."

"That's so nice." Simone took some coins from her pocket. "I'll take a bowl."

Hajrah and her mom appeared at the far side of the reception area. Hajrah ran toward us, waving my notebook. She skidded to a stop in front of the table. There was a bright red rose tucked under her hairband.

"The burglars have been busy," she said. "A bunch of people have had their strawberry plants dug up at night. And there was a nice lady who grows roses as well as strawberries. Her plants were taken, too. Her name is Anne. She gave me this." Hajrah touched the flower in her hair. "She saw something strange the night of the theft."

"What?" I asked.

"An orange bicycle!" Hajrah's eyes went

wide. "She saw two people pushing something orange with wheels through the woods behind her house. She wasn't wearing her glasses, but she's pretty certain it was a bike."

"It could be the bike that left the tread mark outside Mr. Bohdan's garden," I said.

"Exactly!" Hajrah handed me my notebook. "All the details are here."

I opened the notebook. There were four names and addresses. Each name was a gardener who'd lost strawberry plants. Each address was a crime scene. Hajrah was right—the berry burglars had been busy. If we were going to catch them, we needed to get busy, too.

CHAPTER 8

It was raining on Friday morning. When I got to school, wide puddles had already formed on the playground.

The downpour was good for the plants but bad for crime scenes. Four more gardens had been hit by the berry burglars. Each garden had clues I needed to see. If the rain continued, they would all be washed away.

When I got to room 15, Jordan announced that his plaster footprint was ready.

We sat on the carpet with red and yellow circles. Jordan brought over a plastic tray covered by a green towel.

Hajrah stamped her feet. It made a noise like a drumroll.

"I'm so excited to see it!" she said.

"I think it turned out okay. Ready?"

Jordan counted to three and pulled away the green towel. It was like seeing a footprint in reverse. The mold looked like a foot-shaped hill rising out of the piece of plaster.

"When the burglars stepped in the mud," Jordan explained, "they made shallow foot-shaped holes. Most of the footprints were mushed. But I found one that wasn't squished and poured the wet plaster of paris into it. The plaster dried in the exact shape of the footprint."

Hajrah leaned in. "You can even see the tread of the culprit's shoe!"

I moved closer. A pattern of wavy lines crossed the footprint from side to side. Near the middle, the pattern was broken up by a picture.

"Why is there a drawing of a turtle shell on the mold?" I asked.

"They're Turtle rain boots!" Hajrah said. "I have a pair of those. They are so comfortable and always keep my feet dry."

"So the berry burglars were wearing rain boots, not shoes," I said.

"Makes sense if you're going to be walking

through people's muddy gardens," Glitch said. She put her foot beside the mold.

"Your foot is bigger," Jordan said.

"That means one of the burglars has small feet. We need to find out which one of our suspects has feet that small."

"How can we do that?" Jordan asked.

"First we identify the suspects." I picked up my notebook and reviewed my notes. "We know from the hat found in Mr. Bohdan's garden that one of the burglars goes to our school."

"And don't forget the Junior Growers' Club pin," Hajrah said. "It didn't lead us to the burglar, but it means that whoever did this likes to garden."

I nodded. "Yes. I think one of the burglars is a member of the school garden club."

Jordan's eyebrows went up. "You think it was an inside job?"

"The possibility can't be ruled out," I said. "It took gardening skills to dig those plants out with the roots. The burglars want to keep the plants alive."

"So start the search with the people who have the know-how." Jordan smiled. "That's genius, Myron."

"No, just logical."

Hajrah hopped onto her ball and began to bounce. "Okay, let's start with Lauren. She was upset when she wasn't allowed to plant her flowers in the sunniest spot. She could have small feet."

"And she changed the subject when we asked her about being upset," I added.

"I noticed that, too!" Hajrah stopped

bouncing. "She brought up Jessie Sanders and those erasers. Can you believe he denied stealing them for the whole school year?"

"Maybe Jessie is up to his old tricks again," Glitch said.

"He definitely has a bad temper," Hajrah agreed. "Did you see how he snapped at Aaron at the school garden the other day?"

"Maybe Jessie is really mad at the neighborhood strawberry plants, so he's stealing them." Jordan grinned.

"Very funny, Mr. Comedian." Hajrah resumed bouncing on her ball. "I'd still like to know how big his feet are."

I added Jessie's name to the list of suspects.

"The only other club leaders are Umair and Simone," Glitch said.

I looked up from my notebook. "Simone is

not a suspect."

Glitch arched her left eyebrow. "Why not? Can't the client also be the culprit?"

"Ooh, plot twist!" Hajrah said.

"No plot twist," I said. "Simone isn't the burglar because she would have to pretend she didn't do it. And she's not good at pretending. Just like me."

"Okay, we'll rule out Simone," Hajrah said. "That leaves Umair."

"Don't forget he's also on the baseball team with Paulo." Earlier I had told Hajrah and the others about seeing Umair at practice.

"And we know the players aren't happy about having the garden in their outfield," Hajrah said.

"Umair could have helped Paulo take the plants," I suggested.

"We need to get the shoe sizes of those two guys, plus Lauren and Jessie." Hajrah counted each one off on her fingers. "Those four are the suspects."

"They're all in the older grades," Jordan said. "There's no way we can get their shoe sizes without making them suspicious."

"Yes, there is!" Hajrah jumped to her feet and twirled to face Mr. Harpel. "I have an idea for my data management project for math. I'm going to ask all the kids in seventh and eighth grade for their shoe sizes. Then I'll make a graph from their answers for my project. But really I'll be finding out the shoe sizes of all our suspects!"

"And no one will suspect a thing, because you asked everybody," Jordan said. "Now that is *real* genius."

I had to agree. It was a very good plan.

"Solving two problems with one math question," Mr. Harpel said. "I like it. And I'm guessing you want to do that now?"

"You bet!" Hajrah bounced to her desk and got her math notebook and a pencil. "The case won't solve itself."

"Very true," Mr. Harpel chuckled. "Jordan, why don't you join her? You and Hajrah can work on the math problem together."

Hajrah and Jordan ran out of room 15 to start their investigation. Glitch opened her laptop. I went to my table and flipped through my notebook until I found the addresses of the berry burglars' other victims. Four gardens had been robbed. Add the school garden and Mr. Bohdan's backyard, and that meant I had plenty of crime scenes. With the garden club leaders and the baseball team, I had a lot of suspects, too. What I didn't have was a motive. Why were people committing these crimes? Why take only strawberry plants? Why not steal lettuce and carrots, too? The thieves dug up the whole plant, roots and all. Why did they want to keep them alive? If I

couldn't answer all those "whys," I didn't have a motive. Without a motive, this case didn't make sense, and I couldn't solve it.

Mr. Harpel sat in the chair next to my table.

"Myron, you're glaring at your notebook like it's your worst enemy."

"That's impossible," I said. "A notebook can't be my...oh, I see. You're joking."

"In a way I was." Mr. Harpel smiled. "What I meant was that you don't look happy about your discoveries. But it seems to me that you and Hajrah are getting closer to catching the thieves. I would have thought you'd be happy about that."

"I am, I guess. But I feel like we're missing something." I jabbed my pencil at the addresses. "The burglars have stolen strawberries from each of these gardens."

"So the school garden wasn't their only target," Mr. Harpel said.

"True. But why did they take all those plants?" I said. "I wish I could visit these crime scenes. Even with this rain, there might be some clues waiting to be found."

Mr. Harpel read the addresses. "They're not far from here. I recognize the street names."

Glitch looked over from her computer. "Can I see that list? I have an idea."

I handed her the notebook.

"Give me five minutes," she said.

Glitch didn't need five minutes. Three minutes and forty-eight seconds later, she announced she was ready.

"Watch the whiteboard and be amazed!"

The interactive whiteboard lit up with an image from Glitch's laptop. On the screen was a satellite picture of a neighborhood. In the middle was a long patch of green forest. Around the green space were streets and houses. I recognized the place right away.

"That's our neighborhood." I pointed to a
large rectangular building in the middle of
a green field that ran along the edge of the
forest. "There's our school. And that forest is
Warbler Woods."

"You got it," Glitch said. "The arrows over

the houses mark the gardens on your list."

"Ah, now we can see where they all are!" Mr. Harpel said.

Two of the houses were on the same street. The third and fourth houses were on different streets. But all four had one thing in common.

"Each crime scene backs onto Warbler Woods," I said.

"The thieves are using the woods to sneak in and out of the gardens," Glitch said.

"Exactly," I said. "And I bet one of their backyards connects to the woods, too."

Glitch stood in front of the screen. "Somewhere on that map is the home of one of the berry burglars."

CHAPTER 9

Hajrah and Jordan returned just before recess.

"It was a disaster!" Hajrah belly flopped onto her ball and rolled around sadly. "We asked the older kids, including our suspects, but none of them has a shoe size that matches the footprint."

Jordan dropped Hajrah's math notebook on her table. "Everyone has feet much bigger than the mold," he moaned. "Making that mold didn't help us at all."

"Maybe it did," I said. "Mr. Bohdan saw two kids. And there were other footprints on the trail behind his garden." I kneeled next to the mold. "*This* footprint belongs to *one* of the burglars."

"Of course!" Hajrah pushed herself off her ball and landed on the carpet beside me. "The suspects on our list are still our suspects. So this footprint must belong to the second burglar. Someone whose shoe size we didn't get in our survey."

"But we spoke to everyone," Jordan said.

"Not everyone." Hajrah held up a list of the students in seventh and eighth grade. "The teacher gave me a class list. One of the students on it isn't at school today."

"Who?" Glitch asked.

Hajrah grinned. "Lewis Devi."

"He's on the baseball team with Paulo!" Jordan said.

"And he's the smallest kid in seventh grade." I remembered how easily Lewis slipped through the hole in the school fence during baseball practice. Could he be stealing plants with Paulo to get the school garden moved away from their baseball field? It would be an odd way to try to get what they wanted, but a good detective is always open to all possibilities.

"The print could belong to Lewis," Hajrah said. "But I've been thinking about the boot's tread. It has a turtle on it, so we know it's a Turtle brand of boot. Only younger kids like us wear Turtle boots. They don't even make them for older kids. I don't think someone in seventh grade, like Lewis, would wear Turtle boots, even if they did fit him."

"That means one of the berry bandits is our age," I said.

"And that means we need to collect more data!" Hajrah spun to face Mr. Harpel. "Can we interview the kids in the third grade classes?"

Mr. Harpel chuckled. "You'd better hurry. Recess will begin soon."

This time, I joined Hajrah and Jordan. But when we got to the third grade classrooms, our great idea turned out to be a dud.

"Look at all those boots," Hajrah moaned.

Rows of rain boots ran along the walls outside the classrooms. Most of the students had worn boots today because of the rain.

"They're all about the same size as the mold," Jordan said.

Hajrah lifted a boot and checked the sole. She put it down and checked another and then another.

"And they're all Turtle boots!" She frowned.

My stomach tightened. There was no reason to survey the third grade students now. Not only did most of them have the same size foot as the print in the mold, but they all had the same brand of boot. We'd have to track down the berry burglars another way.

We arrived back in room 15 just as the recess bell rang. Mr. Harpel ushered us out.

"The rain has stopped. Go outside. Run around. Be free!"

Mr. Harpel always told us to "run around and be free" at recess. I didn't feel like running. And my mind could not be free until we had caught the burglars.

Hajrah and I walked around the schoolyard, avoiding the other kids and their noise. We stopped at the garden. No one was there— only the vegetable plants and flowers growing quietly in the sun. Simone had filled in the holes where the strawberry plants had been. No trace remained of the crime.

I walked to the chain-link fence at the edge of the yard. On the other side, the trees of Warbler Woods climbed high into the sky. Part of the fence had broken free from its post. I pulled it back and created a small opening.

"The burglars must have come and gone through here," I said. "The same way Lewis crawled through to get the baseball."

"Everybody knows about that hole," Hajrah said. "I see Smasher and her friends crawl through all the time."

"Why doesn't Mr. V. fix it?"

"He does, but the older kids just break it again." Hajrah shrugged. "Older kids are weird."

I peered through the hole into the darkness of the forest. A narrow path led from the fence deep into the woods. It looked just like the trail leading from Mr. Bohdan's backyard.

"If we followed this trail, we could walk to all the gardens that have been hit by the burglars."

"We don't have time," Hajrah said. "Recess will be over soon."

"Maybe we can do it after school?"

She shook her head. "I can't. I have swimming, and I'm not allowed to miss a lesson."

"That's okay," I said. "I just remembered I have to go shopping for summer clothes with my mom. But we have to check out the crime scenes soon. Today is Friday, and tomorrow is the Strawberry Festival. We're running out of time."

The recess bell rang. Hajrah and I walked back to the school. With each step, I knew I was getting farther away from solving this mystery. The berry burglars had walked through the forest to sneak into people's gardens. If I wanted to solve this case, I needed to find a way to do some forest walking, too.

Our chance came at lunchtime. Hajrah and I ate our sandwiches quickly and were the first out the doors for lunch recess.

"We have forty-five minutes to explore the woods," Hajrah said as we raced to the fence. "It's not much time, but it's all we have."

I ran alongside my friend. "I'm still not sure

this is a good idea."

"Of course it's not a good idea," she said. "But you said yourself that we have to see those gardens before tomorrow's Strawberry Festival. This is the only way we can do it."

We got to the fence and Hajrah lifted the broken piece. No one else was around. The other kids and the duty teachers were still just coming out of the school.

"Hurry!" she hissed.

I crawled through. Hajrah scrambled after me.

She jumped to her feet and looked around. "Isn't this exciting?"

"No," I snapped. "We're breaking the school rules. I don't like breaking the rules."

"We'll be back before the end of recess. No one is going to know—not even Mr. Harpel."

Questions swirled through my mind. What if we got lost? What if we took too long and got back late? Hajrah would laugh if I asked these questions out loud. She'd tell me to relax and push my worries aside. But I couldn't. Like the buzzing PA speaker, the questions demanded my attention.

Hajrah stepped closer. Her smile was gone.

"Myron, we don't have to do this if you don't want to." Her words were quiet and calm. "We can find another way to see the gardens."

"No. I can do this." The questions still raced around my brain. They still made my heart pound. But I wasn't going to let them stop me. "Sometimes a detective has to take a risk to crack a case."

"Exactly!" Hajrah's smile returned. "Let's go." She pulled a piece of paper from her pocket and unfolded it. It was a map of the forest and the houses around it. Jordan had drawn it for us when we told him our plan. He'd marked each house that had lost strawberry plants with an X. Hajrah put her finger on the X farthest from the school.

"Let's start there and work our way back."

The canopy of leaves high above us blocked out much of the sunlight. Shadows stretched across the plants and bushes on either side of the trail. With each step along the narrow path, the woods around us grew darker.

Hajrah studied Jordan's map as she walked. "Almost there."

Just then, branches snapped loudly not far from the path. I stopped.

"What was that?"

"Probably just a squirrel," Hajrah whispered.

"Let's keep moving."

"It sounds too big for a squirrel," I said.

Beyond the bushes, an animal growled.

Hajrah stopped walking and turned around. "Okay, that's not a squirrel."

The bushes shook as if they were uprooting themselves.

"It's coming this way," Hajrah hissed. "Hide!"

I couldn't hide. I couldn't even move. The buzzing in my brain spread to my toes and held me frozen on the muddy path. All I could do was wait to be eaten.

CHAPTER 10

A furry head pushed through the bushes.

Two big eyes stared at me. A wet nose sniffed my leg. A warm tongue licked my hand.

A little spotted dog stood at my feet. The buzzing in my brain slowed down. The dog was about the size of a soccer ball and just as harmless. Its owner stepped out from the bushes. She was not harmless.

"Rosebud likes you, Myron!" Smasher

McGintley held a dog leash in one hand.

I stepped away from Rosebud. "She scared me."

"She scared me, too!" Hajrah stepped out from her hiding spot.

Smasher chuckled and rubbed the dog's head.

"It's not funny, Smasher," Hajrah growled. "We thought we were going to get hurt."

"Relax, detectives. Rosebud wouldn't harm a fly." Smasher snapped the leash onto the dog's collar. "She thought you guys wanted to play."

Rosebud licked Smasher's hand. She didn't look scary anymore.

"What are you doing in the woods?" I asked.

Smasher's eyes narrowed. "I go home for lunch, Mr. Detective, so I can take Rosebud out for a walk. She likes to run through the woods."

"And through people's gardens," Hajrah
snapped. "Like when you and your friends
threw sticks into Mr. Bohdan's vegetable patch
and sent Rosebud in to get them. She trampled
the poor man's plants."

Smasher's lips curled into a sneer. "How did
you know about that?"

"Mr. Bohdan told us," I said. "He saw
someone stealing his strawberry plants."

"And since you're always making trouble, he thinks it's you," Hajrah added.

"That old man needs to get his eyes checked," Smasher snorted. "Whoever he saw, it wasn't me. Leave me out of your little detective games." She tugged on Rosebud's leash. "See you later, snoops."

When Smasher was gone, Hajrah picked up Jordan's map and wiped off the dirt. She had dropped it when Rosebud startled us. "We still need to get to the first garden," she said.

Hajrah hurried down the path. I followed. I kept my eyes on the bushes, just in case Rosebud—or something worse—jumped out at us again. I had no doubt that Smasher would think it was hilarious to circle back and scare us twice.

After a few minutes of walking in silence, I

stopped at a break in the bushes.

"Hurry up, Myron!" Hajrah called. "We don't have time to stop and look at the flowers."

"I'm not looking at flowers," I said. "I found something."

A second trail ran off the main one. It was much narrower and not as well traveled. A familiar-looking groove ran the length of it. Hajrah ran back to me and saw the groove.

"A bike track!" she gasped. "Change of plans. Let's see where this leads!"

The path snaked toward the houses that stood at the edge of the woods. The tire-track groove definitely looked like the one we'd found near Mr. Bohdan's garden. The berry burglars must have used a bike to move the stolen plants. My heart beat faster. We were getting close.

Ahead of me, Hajrah stopped. "What's that?"

She charged off the path. Five seconds later, she returned, pushing an orange wheelbarrow.

"Look what I found hidden under the bushes!"

"A wheelbarrow."

"Nope." She grinned. "An orange bike."

"That's not an orange bike."

"I know that, Myron," Hajrah said, still grinning. "But this could be what Anne saw."

"The lady from the botanical gardens?"

"Yes, the one who gave me the rose, remember?" Hajrah bounced next to the wheelbarrow. "She thought the burglars were pushing an orange bike. But she didn't have her glasses on. All she could see was something orange with wheels."

"But that has just one wheel, not two."

"I know, but watch this." Hajrah pushed the wheelbarrow into the groove. The fat wheel sunk in easily. "It fits! I knew it would."

"So Anne saw the thieves pushing a wheelbarrow, not a bike," I said. "The berry burglars must have put the stolen plants into the wheelbarrow to carry them away."

"That's what I was thinking." Hajrah studied the trail closely.

Footprints covered the muddy ground. The prints had

a wavy tread and were clear enough to make out the Turtle boot logo.

"They match Jordan's plaster mold," Hajrah announced. "And there are more!"

Next to the Turtle boot prints was another set of footprints. They had a tread made up of little circles.

"These prints were made by a different pair of boots," Hajrah said. "And they are larger."

"The second berry burglar is bigger and probably older," I said. "That means they're not classmates."

Hajrah tugged on her braid. "Why would two kids from different grades work together to steal strawberry plants?"

"I have no idea," I said.

"At least we know the berry burglars definitely came this way."

Hajrah returned the wheelbarrow to where she found it, and we continued up the path. The wheelbarrow track ran right up to an old wooden gate. A thick hedge, twice as tall as me, grew on either side.

"There's a backyard on the other side of that hedge," Hajrah said.

"So the berry burglars came this far," I said.

"That's true." Hajrah looked around. She studied Jordan's map. "But the nearest crime scene is at the far end of the woods. This isn't one of the yards we're looking for."

"Or maybe it's exactly what we're looking for," I said. "The thieves could have struck here last night and we wouldn't know about it yet."

"Do you think there's a fresh crime scene through this gate?" Hajrah's eyes widened.

"That would be way better than the other gardens we're looking for."

"Everything would be just as the thieves left it," I said.

"And that means more clues for us." She pushed on the gate, and it swung open. "But we have to be quick. Lunch recess will be over soon."

We stepped into a small backyard. There was a brick house with a wide wooden deck. A garden covered most of the yard. There were no holes in the soil and no missing plants. We were wrong. This wasn't a crime scene.

But I had never been so happy to be wrong.

"Strawberries!" Hajrah gasped.

It was a fruit garden. And it had only one kind of fruit. Plump red strawberries grew all over the yard. Straight rows of strawberry

plants flourished in the garden's dark soil. Berries overflowed from several large pots.

"We've found the stolen plants." Hajrah danced on the spot. "The mystery is solved!"

"The mystery is *almost* solved," I corrected. I wasn't ready to celebrate just yet.

These strawberries had to be the ones taken by the berry burglars. A trail of clues had led us to this backyard, but they didn't tell the whole story. There was no motive for the crimes. Why steal strawberries when you can buy them at the store? Why bring all the plants to one spot and plant them? Without a motive, this mystery wouldn't be completely solved.

A banner hung over the deck, strung up between two posts. I hadn't noticed it when I first came into the yard. It was like the kind you get for a birthday party. Something was written on it in big letters. I walked around to the front of the banner to see. It read: "Welcome Home, Mom!"

At last, it all made sense. The berry thefts, the strawberry-filled garden, and the banner—it all came together to explain why this had happened. Finally, there was a motive.

"Myron, why are you smiling?" Hajrah asked.

"Because now the mystery *is* solved." I walked quickly back to the gate.

She followed. "You know who the berry burglars are?"

"And I know *why* they did it," I said. "And if we want to catch them, we need to get back to school right away."

CHAPTER 11

The bell rang just as we crawled back under the fence.

Across the yard, children ran to the school. Hajrah and I didn't run to class. We had somewhere else to go.

"I knew it couldn't have been Paulo and the baseball team," Hajrah said. "Stealing a few strawberry plants wouldn't get the garden moved from their outfield. And Lauren didn't really seem too bothered that Simone's plants got the sunniest spot, so none of the evidence pointed to her."

We hurried to the front of the school.

"Are you sure they'll be there?" Hajrah asked.

I checked my watch. It was almost 12:45.

"They'll be there," I said. "Just like they've been there every day this week."

When we rounded the corner, the berry burglars stood at the school doors, looking out at the parking lot. Their backpacks lay at their feet.

"Is your dad late?"

Jessie and Aaron Sanders jumped at the sound of my voice.

"How did you know we were waiting for our dad?" Aaron asked.

"You've left class at this time every day this week," Hajrah said.

"We know you go to visit your mom in the hospital," I added.

"We also know about the strawberry plants."

Jessie's eyes narrowed. "What are you talking about?"

"We saw your garden," I explained. "We know you've been sneaking into people's yards at night while your dad is at the hospital with your mom."

"We know you dug up the strawberry plants and brought them back to your yard in an orange wheelbarrow." Hajrah pointed to Aaron's feet. They were about the same size as mine. "Those are Turtle boots, aren't they? We have a footprint cast that will match the treads on those boots and place you at the scene of the crime, Aaron."

The younger boy's eyes dropped to his feet.

Jessie glared at us but didn't say a word.

"And we have this." I held the Junior Growers' Club pin in my hand. Aaron froze when he saw it. "It fell off when you dropped your school baseball cap in Mr. Bohdan's backyard."

"How do you know it's mine?" Aaron asked.

"You were looking for something in your desk on Wednesday. Something green," I said. "At first, I didn't realize it was a hat. But that's what you were searching for, wasn't it?"

He looked at the ground and nodded.

Hajrah stepped closer to Jessie. "And I know why you were so mad at your brother when he came to the school garden the morning after Simone's strawberries were stolen. You'd told him to stay away from the crime scene. But he didn't listen. You were scared we'd figure it out."

"And that's exactly what we've done," I said.

"Face it, guys. We know you're the berry burglars."

"And we know why you did it," I added.

A car pulled into the school drive. The boys watched nervously as it got closer. Their dad was behind the wheel. Their mother sat beside him. Angie Sanders—the woman who loved strawberries so much that her friends at the botanical gardens sold bowls of them to raise money to buy her a gift.

"Your mom was too sick to grow her own berries this season," I said.

"The yard looked so sad without Mom there to take care of the plants," Jessie said finally. "We wanted to do something special for her when she got out of the hospital."

"We wanted to fill the yard with strawberries," Aaron explained. "But we didn't have any money to buy plants."

"So you decided to steal them?" Hajrah asked.

"We only took a few plants from each garden!" Jessie said.

"We hoped people wouldn't notice," Aaron added.

"You left holes in people's yards!" Hajrah laughed. "They noticed all right, and they're upset. They want their plants back."

"You won't tell our parents, will you?" Jessie asked.

"We won't." I shook my head. "You will."

The boys' eyes grew wide.

Hajrah crossed her arms. "Your mom is going to wonder where the strawberry plants came from. I'm surprised your dad hasn't already asked you about them."

Jessie shrugged. "Lately he's been too busy with work and visiting Mom to notice anything."

"We know you did this to help your mom, but she will figure it out," Hajrah said. "You'll be in less trouble if you tell your parents the truth now."

"And return all the plants," I added. "Simone and the other gardeners want them back."

The car pulled up to the curb. Mrs. Sanders stepped out slowly. She looked tired and frail. Aaron ran to his mom and wrapped her in a big hug.

"Simone and the gardeners will all be at the Strawberry Festival tomorrow, Jessie," Hajrah said. "You and Aaron should come and talk to them. Tell them what you did and why. They might understand."

"I doubt it." Jessie turned his back to us and joined the family hug.

My stomach felt tight. This wasn't right. We had caught the berry burglars, but they weren't going to return the stolen plants. This mystery wouldn't be resolved until Simone and the others had their strawberries back.

"I'm going to tell Mr. and Mrs. Sanders what their kids did," I said.

Hajrah put a hand on my shoulder. "That's not a good idea, Myron."

She led me into the school.

"Why did you stop me?" I asked. "We know Jessie and Aaron are guilty, and we know where the plants are. We should have told their parents and closed the case for good."

"Let's give them a chance to do the right thing on their own." Hajrah tugged on her braid. "That's what good detectives would do."

"And we're good detectives," I said.

"We're the best!" Hajrah twirled on the spot.

I smiled at my spinning detective partner. But as we walked to class, the tightness in my stomach didn't go away.

CHAPTER 12

The next morning, I didn't feel like the best detective.

It felt wrong to solve a mystery but not tell anyone about it. I understood why Hajrah wanted to give Jessie and Aaron time to tell their parents the truth. Their mom had been sick for so long, and it wouldn't have been nice of us to bring it up just as they were being reunited. But would the boys confess?

As I got dressed, I remembered what Lauren

had said about Jessie. He'd lied about taking her erasers for a whole year. And even when they were found in his desk, he didn't admit to the crime. Why should we expect him to tell the truth now?

My brain buzzed thinking about Simone and the other people who'd lost their plants. They deserved to get their strawberries back. Jessie and Aaron needed to admit to being the berry burglars, or the West Meadows Detectives would do it for them.

Hajrah and her mom picked me up. We arrived at the botanical gardens just as the Strawberry Festival was getting started. A few tables had been set up on the grass. A band played lively music and a crowd had already gathered to admire the fresh strawberries, jams, and pies.

"I'm surprised you two wanted to come here on a Saturday morning," Mrs. Badour said. "I didn't know you liked strawberries so much."

"Strawberries are nice," Hajrah agreed. "But seeing a mystery get solved is even better."

"I don't understand," Mrs. Badour said.

"Hopefully you will very soon," I said.

Mrs. Badour looked at us and shook her head.

"I honestly don't know what you children are talking about half the time." She waved to someone. "There's Maureen from work. I'm going to say hello."

Hajrah and I spotted Simone chatting to the women from the other day. They were dishing out more fresh berries to a line of eager customers. We had spoken to Simone yesterday after school and told her about finding the strawberry plants in Jessie and Aaron's backyard. We also told her about confronting the brothers. She agreed with our decision not to tell their parents. But I think she was having doubts, like me.

"Have you seen them?" she asked when she came over.

"Not yet." Hajrah sighed. "If Jessie and Aaron just showed up, told the truth, and returned the plants, the gardeners they stole from might not be too upset."

"Telling the truth is hard sometimes for Jessie," Simone said.

She looked over to the tables on the grass. All the gardeners from the seed swap sat in the morning sun. Hajrah waved to a lady with a rose in her hair. The lady waved back.

"That's Anne," Hajrah said. "She's the one who gave me the rose. And Mr. Bohdan is here, too!"

My brain buzzed again when I saw Mr. Bohdan and the other gardeners. They had all been hurt by Jessie and Aaron. And now it seemed as if the two of them weren't even going to show up and tell the truth.

"This isn't right," I said. "We solved this mystery, we found the plants, and now we're protecting the culprits? That is not what detectives do. I'm going to tell Mr. Bohdan and the others what happened."

I started marching to the picnic tables.

"Myron, slow down!" Hajrah called. "Maybe they need a little more time."

I didn't slow down. I kept walking until I stood right in front of Mr. Bohdan and the other gardeners. The old man looked up.

"Here are our detectives now!" Mr. Bohdan smiled. "Any news on our missing plants?"

"Big news," I said.

"I think we should wait," Hajrah whispered beside me.

I ignored her and took a deep breath.

"Attention, strawberry gardeners," I said in

a loud voice.

My mouth went dry when I saw them looking at me. I don't like speaking to groups of people. But sometimes detectives have to do uncomfortable things. I took another deep breath.

"My detective partner and I have found your plants."

The gardeners cheered.

"And we know who took them."

"Who did it?" a lady in a wide-brimmed hat called from one of the tables.

"We did."

The voice came from behind me.

I turned to see Aaron and Jessie walking toward the picnic tables, each holding a strawberry plant in a brown pot.

"My brother and I took your plants,"

Jessie said. "We wanted to help our mom feel better."

"But we ended up hurting all of you," Aaron said. "We're sorry."

Their family's car was parked at the curb. An open-topped trailer was attached to the back. In it were the stolen strawberry plants. Mr. and Mrs. Sanders watched their sons.

"We brought all the plants back," Aaron said. "We took good care of them and saved all the berries for you."

Mr. Bohdan got to his feet. He and the other gardeners hurried over to the trailer.

Hajrah and I watched as the boys apologized to every gardener and returned each person's strawberry plants.

"They finally owned up to their crime." Hajrah wiggled her eyebrows. "Anything you'd like to say to me, detective partner?"

"You were right," I admitted. "Jessie and Aaron just needed time to do the right thing."

"Thank you." Hajrah twirled on the spot. Her braid whizzed around and brushed my cheek. It felt like a tickle.

"Thank *you*," I said. "You showed me there's more to being a detective than just solving mysteries."

Simone walked back from the trailer carrying a strawberry plant. She brought it close to her nose, breathed in deeply, and smiled.

"Thank you for all your help, detectives." She picked two plump strawberries and handed them to us. "Go on, taste the fruits of your success."

Hajrah bit into the strawberry. Red juice

rolled down her chin.

"Delicious!" she said.

I bit into my berry and savored the sweet
taste of a mystery solved.

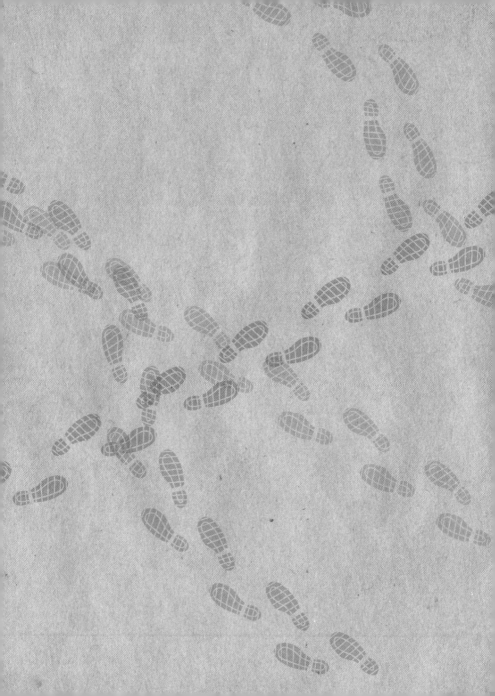